MORE *to r*

D0394120

To Bobbi

Trilby

a bird in my hat

written and illustrated by
Paul Adshead

Child's Play (International) Ltd
Swindon   Bologna   New York

*Dedicated to my family, but in particular to my father.
Thank you for your kindness, patience and generosity,
and for inventing such wonderful bed-time stories.*

Chapter One

A New Project

The school bell rang and everybody cheered.

"Enjoy the holidays, children," shouted Mrs Carter, trying to make herself heard over the excited chatter and loud slamming of desk lids. "And don't forget to do your homework!"

"Hurry up, Ben," said Mrs Carter, her voice echoing round the empty classroom. "Stop dawdling or you'll miss the bus."

Picking up my satchel, I trudged towards the door.

"Whatever's the matter?" asked Mrs Carter. "Aren't you looking forward to having a whole week off school?"

"No," I replied gloomily. "Not much."

"But it's Spring!" Mrs Carter exclaimed. "The loveliest time of the year. Everyone enjoys the Spring holidays."

That was the problem. I never enjoyed the Spring holidays. Spring means two things in our house, and both of them mean **trouble**.

My first problem is **spring cleaning**!

My mother is the **fussiest** mother in the world.
She is the kind of mother who spring cleans
every single week: not just in spring,
but summer, autumn and winter too!
That's bad enough, but during the Spring holidays
she goes absolutely mad. She zooms round the house
like a human whirlwind until each room pongs
of pine disinfectant. And to make matters worse,
I have to spring clean my bedroom
while she supervises!

My other problem
is **gardening**!

My Dad is the world's keenest gardener.
Every Spring holiday he takes the week off work
(supposedly so we can all go on picnics
and have days out), but instead, he spends
the whole time weeding, hoeing, digging
and planting.
And whenever I sneak out of the house
to escape Mum, Dad catches me
and I have to help him instead!

I explained my problems to Mrs Carter.
"Cheer up!" she said. "Things could be worse.
My Dad was a farmer. When I was your age,
I had to get up at five o'clock every morning
and help him milk the cows!"
I tried to imagine what Mrs Carter looked like
when she was my age.

I'm always imagining things.
Sometimes I imagine
people as animals.
Mum looks just like
a fussy little chicken.

Dad reminds me
of a short,
stumpy beaver
with sticking-out teeth!

"Stop daydreaming," said Mrs Carter.
"Come along, Ben. If you help me carry these books
to my car, I'll give you a lift home."

Later, as we rattled along the road
in Mrs Carter's old Morris Minor,
we chatted about the holiday homework.

"Do you remember the nature notebook I did
during the last holidays?" I asked.

"Of course," she replied. "You wrote all about
the hedgehog you secretly cared for.
It was the best in the class.
I hope the 'Bird-Spotting Diary' you're doing
these holidays will be just as good."

"That's another problem," I replied.
"Mum still won't let me have any pets,
and Dad tries to scare birds out of the garden,
because they eat all the seed he plants
before it gets a chance to grow.
I probably won't spot any birds at all."

"Never mind," laughed Mrs Carter as she pulled up
at my gate. "I expect something will turn up!"

She was right. Something did.
Something very unexpected indeed!

Bird-Spotting Diary

Friday May 3rd

5.30 p.m.

I sat outside, until tea was ready, on the look-out for any birds in or around the garden.

There were a few sparrows having a dust-bath in the vegetable plot and a robin hopping about under the hedge. A seagull flew over, and I could hear the sound of rooks cawing from the big trees in Coppin Field.

Best news of all – I think a pair of pigeons are nesting in the ivy below the bathroom window. My mother can't have noticed them because the bathroom windows have frosted glass!

Chapter Two

A Baby Pigeon

The following morning, the sun shone brightly
in a clear blue sky. While I ate my breakfast,
Mum and Dad argued.

"Ben can help me with the weeding this morning,"
said my father with his mouth full of toast,
spraying crumbs over the table.

Mum glared at him and started flicking
at the table cloth with her napkin.
"No, Ben is helping me," she insisted.
"Some filthy bird has done a Billy Bonga all over
the bathroom window. I can't wash just that window,
it'll make all the others look dirty. I'll have to
wash them all. Ben can fetch the buckets of water
and steady the ladder."

We did the front of the house first,
then the back. I was so hot by the time
we got round to the dreaded bathroom window,
that I completely forgot about the pigeons
nesting there.

Dad leaned the ladder against the bathroom
window-sill.
Then, as Mother climbed up carrying the bucket
and brush, he took off his hat
and mopped his forehead with his hanky.
"I wish I could have a nice cold shower,"
he groaned.

Suddenly, just as Mother reached the top,
two grey pigeons shot out of the ivy
and zoomed past her head.
She gave a scream that a peacock
would have been proud of,
and promptly dropped her bucket and brush
as she clutched at the ladder to stop herself
from falling off.

The brush bounced into the pigeons' nest
and sent the whole pile of twigs and leaves
cascading to the ground, while the bucket landed
right on poor Dad's head, drenching him
in ice-cold water.

"It looks like your wish has come true,"
laughed Mother as she descended.
"Stand on the grass, dear. You're dripping
all over my nice clean path."

I took hold of poor old Dad's hat while
he removed the bucket and rubbed his bruised head.
Then, as I was about to hand it back,
I had the surprise of my life.

There, in the bottom of the hat, was the smallest
and probably the ugliest little creature
I have ever seen.
It was about three centimetres long,
fleshy pink with a few sprigs
of bright yellow down, and had a beak
that was much too big
for its tiny head.

"It must be a baby pigeon!" I gasped.

"Well, it looks hideous," said my mother.
"Stick the revolting creature
back in its nest at once."

"But it hasn't got a nest any longer," I replied,
pointing to the twigs and leaves
scattered over the path.
"The poor thing must have fallen into the hat
when you broke the nest and knocked it out."

"I did no such thing," Mother snapped,
looking just a little guilty.
"Leave it on the lawn, so it can go and look
for its parents."

My mother's complete ignorance
when it comes to the subject of wildlife
never ceases to astonish me.

"But it's far too young to be able to fly
and can't possibly be able to feed itself,"
I said, trying to be patient.
"Apart from that, its parents are probably
half-way to the next county by now."

Then, taking advantage of the fact that Mum
was beginning to look guilty, I announced,
"I'll have to try and feed it,
until it's big enough to look after itself."

Mum was forced to give in.
"Well, as long as you don't bring it
into the house," she said, looking even guiltier.
Then after glaring at the twigs round her feet,
she added, "Look at the mess it's made already.
Mark my words – that creature will be nothing
but trouble!"

"You can keep it in my shed," said Dad
with a kindly wink.

"Very well, Ben," said Mother in a frosty voice.
"You may keep it, but as soon as it's old enough
to care for itself, **it has to go**!"

"You can't blame it for **this** mess," laughed Dad.
"Anyway, I don't see how a little bird like that
can cause **any** trouble."

"Don't you indeed," Mother replied with a snort.
"Perhaps this will wipe the smile off your face –
it's just done a huge Billy Bonga in your hat!"

Bird-Spotting Diary

Saturday May 4th

11.45 a.m.

Mother accidentally knocked a baby pigeon
out of its nest, so I will have to hand-rear it.
As it will need a nest, I've done some research
in my wildlife encyclopaedia
on the subject of nest-building.

A nest provides shelter and protection
for the nestling. There are different kinds
of nests. Some (like a blackbird's)
are called 'cup' nests because of their shape.
Swallows make 'bracket' nests out of mud
on the sides of buildings.
Some water birds make 'raft' nests.

All kinds of materials may be used
for nest-building, such as sticks, heather,
seaweed, grass, moss, leaves, wool, hair,
feathers, cobwebs, mud, bones, and even droppings!

I don't think pigeons must be very good
nest-builders. Their nests seem very flimsy.
I'll have to see if I can do any better!

Chapter Three

Trilby gets his Name

I carried my baby pigeon
to the shed and left it
sitting safely inside
Dad's hat, while I got busy
trying to make a nest.

First of all, I picked up
all the old leaves and twigs
that had been part of its original nest.
Next, I gathered a few more useful bits and pieces.
Then I tried weaving them together
into the right shape.
It was absolutely hopeless.
It kept falling apart all the time,
and in the end I had to give up.

"Birds must be really clever," I said to Dad,
when he popped into the shed
to see how I was managing.
"They make their nests
just using one beak,
and I can't do it
with two hands!"

"You don't need to make
a nest," laughed Dad.
"He's already got
a perfectly good one."

"What do you mean?" I asked.

"The hat, of course," he replied. "It's about the right size and shape. It's warm and cosy. Anyway, I don't fancy wearing it again," he added. "He's done several more Billy Bongas in it!"

"You're right, Dad!" I exclaimed. "It makes a perfect nest. I can line it with tissues that can be changed when they get dirty. Are you sure you don't mind?"

He laughed. "I don't think a trilby suits me. Have you decided what to call him yet?"

I tried to think of a name for my new pet while I was nest-building, but nothing I thought of suited him. Suddenly I had a brilliant idea. "I know," I said. "I'll call him Trilby – like your hat!"

Dad thought it was the perfect name. Then he reminded me that, although Trilby had a comfortable nest, he would soon be hungry, so I'd better find out what to feed him. "Perhaps he'll eat worms," he suggested.

"I don't think so," I replied. "I think adult pigeons eat seed, but I'm not sure about babies."

"Why don't you go to the library before it closes?" said Dad. "They'll have some books about pigeons."

Then he gave me fifty pence, in case I needed to buy food from the pet shop.

"Thanks, Dad!" I shouted as I hurried off. "Watch Trilby until I get back."

Bird-Spotting Diary

Saturday May 4th

12.30 p.m.

I have just been reading about young pigeons
in a library book. It says that the eggs hatch
after eighteen days. Baby pigeons
are called squeakers. For the first few days
the parent pigeons feed their squeakers
a substance called 'Pigeon Milk'. Pigeon milk
is formed in the crop. The crop is a bag-like part
of the pigeon's throat, where food is broken up
for digestion before passing into the stomach.

After a few days the squeakers are also fed
on partly digested corn. The parent pigeons
feed their squeakers by regurgitation.
That means that the squeaker puts its beak
into its parent's mouth and the parent brings back
the softened corn from its crop, and puts it
directly down the squeaker's throat.

Doesn't it sound disgusting?
I can't see how I'm going
to manage anything like that.
From the pictures in the book,
I think Trilby is about a week old,
so softened corn
should be the right food.

Chapter Four

Feeding Troubles

I hurried back home with my bag of corn.
I spooned some into a jar of warm water and left
it to soak for a while. When it seemed soft enough,
I fetched Trilby, who was fast asleep in his hat.

I thought about the way his real parents
would have fed him, and wondered what would be
the best way to feed him myself.
I tried to prise his beak open with one hand,
while with the other I dropped tiny bits of corn
in his gaping mouth. It was very fiddly,
and not at all successful. He kept closing
his beak at the wrong time, and I ended up
with more corn on the floor than in his mouth!

He seemed very weak
and tired now,
and I knew that
if he didn't get
a good meal soon,
he would probably die.

I placed him gently on the palm of my hand
and held him close to my face.
"What am I going to do with you?" I whispered.

Suddenly both his eyes opened wide, he lifted
his head and thrust his beak into the corner
of my mouth. Then he started to flap his puny
little wing stumps and made hungry squeaks.

I could hardly believe it.
Obviously he wanted to be fed
in the same way
as his parents
would have fed him.
The idea didn't appeal
to me very much,
but what else
could I do?
I placed
a spoonful
of the soggy corn
into my mouth,
and held him up
to my face again.

Once more, he stuck his beak into my mouth
and opened it wide. Then, with my tongue, I pushed
the food into his throat and he swallowed it.

It had worked, but he was still flapping
his wing stumps and making squeaking noises.

"Now I know why baby pigeons are called squeakers!"
I laughed. Then I placed another spoonful of corn
in my mouth. This time Trilby got so excited,
he almost popped his whole head into my mouth.

At that very moment Mother opened the shed door.

She stared at me in astonishment, and for a second
I thought she was going to faint. Instead, she gave
another of her tremendous screams and galloped
back up the garden path like a race horse!

"Harold, **Harold**!" she cried. "Come quickly!
Ben's so hungry, he's trying to eat the pigeon!"

Bird-Spotting Diary

Saturday May 4th

1.45 p.m.

I have successfully managed to feed Trilby.
The pigeon book from the library says
that the parents feed their squeakers regularly
from dawn until dusk. The squeakers cannot feed
themselves until they are about five weeks old.

That means that I will have to feed Trilby
every couple of hours, from about five o'clock
each morning until about nine o'clock each evening,
for the next five weeks!

I'm not sure I'd fancy feeding Trilby if squeakers ate
worms!

Chapter Five

A Good Idea

When I went in for lunch, Mother was waiting for me at the kitchen door with my toothbrush and toothpaste in her hand. She made me brush my teeth about a hundred times, then forced me to swill my mouth out with some horrible antiseptic stuff that smelt like the school toilets.

I tried to explain that I hadn't been eating Trilby, but feeding him the only way he was used to.

But Mother was not at all convinced. "I've never seen anything so disgusting in my entire life," she said with a shudder. "It can't be hygienic. Don't ever do it again. **Really**! The sooner that bird goes, the better!"

"There must be
a proper way
to feed him,"
she grumbled, as she
picked up a sponge cake
that had been cooling
on a wire tray.

"Didn't you find anything
in your library book?"
asked Dad.

"No," I sighed,
watching as Mother
mixed the butter-cream
icing for the cake.
"There isn't
any helpful
advice on
hand-rearing pigeons at all."

"Well, you'd better get your thinking-cap on,"
Mother scolded, pouring the icing into her
piping-bag.

I sat there with my head in my hands,
staring at the cake as she started
to decorate it. She steadied the cake
with her left hand, while squeezing
the piping-bag with her right.
Every time she squeezed, the butter-cream icing
oozed out. As I watched, I suddenly had
one of my incredible ideas.

"Oh, by the way, I've just thought of a good way
to feed Trilby," I said casually.
"I can't tell you about it just yet.
Why don't you go and put your feet up for a while,
Mother, dear? I'll do the washing-up for you."

Bird-Spotting Diary

Saturday May 4th

4.00 p.m.

I have just given Trilby his second feed,
but this time I did it differently.

I sort of borrowed Mum's piping bag,
while she was out of the kitchen.
I put a few spoonfuls of soggy corn in it,
and held it in my right hand.
With my left hand I gently held Trilby's beak open.
Then all I had to do was squeeze the piping-bag
and the corn mixture oozed down Trilby's throat.

I think I will have to sneak Trilby
up to my bedroom this evening.
I don't fancy going down to the garden shed
at five o'clock each morning all on my own.
It will be cosier in my room too.
I'm sure he misses the warmth of his Mum
sitting on him to keep him warm.
In the morning I can give him his first two feeds,
then smuggle him out
before my mother and father wake up.

Chapter Six

A Surprise

The first time that I smuggled Trilby
into my bedroom for the night, everything went
according to plan. He slept peacefully
inside the hat, on the bedside table.
I set my alarm clock for five a.m., and put it
under my pillow so that no-one else would hear it.
In the morning, I gave him his first feed
as soon as I woke up, and I went back to sleep
until it was time for his second feed two hours
later. All went well on the second morning too,
but the third morning was a disaster!

It was my own fault. I had been up very late
the night before, reading my library book
about pigeons, and the following morning
I never heard the alarm ringing.

Trilby didn't over-sleep though.
Shortly after five o'clock,
he started making
hungry squeaking noises.
At first he must
have just squeaked quietly,
but when no-one fed him,
his squeaks got louder
and louder,
until it sounded
as if about a hundred mice
were having
a yodelling competition!

Finally, the noise woke me up, but I wasn't
the only one. Just as I started feeding him,
the bedroom door burst open and Mother stormed in,
looking like a grumpy, grizzly bear
and started to give me a telling off!

"Stop that dreadful noise at once!" she began.
Then, seeing that it was Trilby who was the culprit,
she shrieked, "I thought I told you
not to bring that bird into the house!"

I was just about to make some sort of excuse,
when she spotted what I was using to feed Trilby.
"My piping-bag!" she gasped. "How dare you?"
She stood with her hands on her hips
trying to look furious, but for some reason
she suddenly started to laugh.

"That's the funniest thing I've ever seen," she chuckled. "It's a jolly good idea too. But you should have asked me if you could use it first."

I didn't really see what was so funny, but as she seemed in a fairly good mood now, I decided to take advantage of it.

"Don't worry, Mum," I said. "When I get my pocket-money, I'll buy you another one."

Still laughing, she sat down on my bed and watched as I finished feeding Trilby. I told her about the way that adult pigeons feed their young. Then, after I had lined the hat with clean tissue paper, I placed a satisfied little squeaker back inside.

"He's really no trouble at all, once he's been fed," I explained.

"So I see," Mum agreed. "Very well, you can bring him in at night then, as long as he doesn't make that dreadful noise again and always stays inside his hat."

So from then on, Trilby came into the house every evening, and after a day or two, Mum got so used to him that even when I brought him in earlier and earlier, she didn't seem to mind.

On Saturday, she gave me an old feather duster
with the handle broken off.
"Perhaps Trilby would like to snuggle
under this at night," she suggested.
"I suppose it would feel rather like
snuggling under his real mother!"

"Thanks, Mum," I said. "Does this mean
you're starting to like Trilby after all?"

"Maybe," she smiled. "But don't get any ideas
about keeping him."

I plucked up courage and decided to ask
the big question . . .
"Please, Mum," I said, "will you look after
Trilby for me, while I'm at school?"

"You must be joking!" she laughed.
"I don't like him **that** much!
Anyway, it takes all my time to look after you
and your father. Trilby is your responsibility.
He'll have to go to school with you!"

Bird-Spotting Diary

Sunday May 12th

3.15 p.m.

Haven't had chance to do much bird-spotting this week.
I've been too busy hand-rearing my baby pigeon.

Being a parent bird must be hard work.
They have to search for food, but can't stray
too far from the nest.
(I can take my nest with me wherever I go!)

Some birds, like blue tits, keep their nest clean
and tidy by carrying all the nestlings' droppings away.
Pigeons don't bother. Their nests get really messy.
(I'd better not tell Mum about that!)

Very young pigeons don't need to drink.
They get enough moisture from the soggy regurgitated
food.

Chapter Seven

Trilby goes to School

When Monday morning arrived,
I felt excited
and a little bit
nervous too.
Whatever would
Mrs Carter say
when I walked
into her classroom
with a baby pigeon?

I gave Trilby
his nine o'clock feed
fifteen minutes early,
so I wouldn't be late for school.
Then I popped him into the hat,
grabbed my satchel and hurried off.

As I walked along, I talked to Trilby.
He peered out from under his feather duster,
occasionally answering with a high pitched squeak.
He seemed to like the sound of my voice and could
recognize it even when he couldn't see me.

I had been looking after him for a little over
a week, and it was amazing how much he'd grown.
If he stood on tiptoe, he could just manage
to peer out of the hat. The last few tufts
of yellow down had vanished and short,
stubby quills of feathers poked through his
flabby pink skin.

I walked into the classroom, just as the bell rang.
Mrs Carter was sitting at her desk and by her feet,
in a basket,
lay Mitzi her dog.
Mrs Carter often brought
Mitzi to school,
because she got lonely
left at home on her own
all day.

I felt fairly sure that Mrs Carter couldn't object
to one of her pupils bringing a bird to school,
when **she** brought an animal.

I showed Trilby to Mrs Carter. Then I explained
why he had to be with me all the time
and asked if he could stay.

"As long as Trilby behaves himself, he can stay.
It will be an excellent opportunity
for the whole class to learn more about birds."

Mrs Carter helped me move my desk
near to the window, then Trilby's hat was placed
on the window-sill. He was no trouble at all.
He sat in the hat perfectly still and quiet,
except when he heard me answer.
Then he would peep
over the rim of the hat
and give a few hungry squeaks,
making everyone laugh.

"Why does he do that?"
someone asked.

Mrs Carter explained:

"Whenever the parent pigeons return with food, they always call to their nestlings as they land beside the nest. The baby birds learn to recognize the sound of their own parents' voices. Trilby has learned to recognize Ben's voice because he thinks Ben is his mother!"

Everyone laughed but I blushed as red as a strawberry.

"There is a special word for the way a baby bird
learns to recognize its parents," said Mrs Carter.
"Does anybody know what that word is?"

I knew because I remembered reading about it
in my library book.
I was the only one in the whole class
to put my hand up.

"Yes, Ben?" said Mrs Carter.

"Imprinting," I replied.

"Very good," said Mrs Carter.
"For your homework tonight, I want you all
to find out as much as you can about imprinting
and write it down in your 'Bird-Spotting Diaries'."

Bird-Spotting Diary

Monday May 13th

7.30 p.m.

Imprinting is the special word for the way baby birds
and their parents learn to recognize each other.
It can be very important. There may be hundreds of nests
on the side of a cliff, and the mother seagull
has to be able to recognize her own nestlings.

Some baby birds (like ducklings) are strong enough
to leave their nest on the first day. They need to
recognize their mother so they will not follow
the wrong bird when they go out swimming!

Most birds imprint on the first thing they see
when they come out of the egg. When birds are
hand-reared they imprint on their human parents.

I have a picture book about imprinting.
It is called *The Chicken That Could Swim.*
It is about a duckling that is hatched by a chicken
which grows up thinking the chicken is her mother.
Then one day she falls into a pond and meets all her real
brothers and sisters! I'm taking it to school tomorrow,
so Mrs Carter can read it to the whole class.

Chapter Eight

Imprinting and Instinct

The rest of that week went by without any trouble.
Trilby settled into our daily routine and seemed
to enjoy coming to school with me.

He was still growing quite quickly, and short,
stubbly quills of feathers were sprouting
out of his skin. The last few tufts
of yellow down had vanished and it looked as if
he was going to be mostly white with brownish-grey
patches over his wings. He was large enough
to clamber right out of the hat now,
whenever he wanted to. So I had to make sure
I took him with me wherever I went,
or he'd try to follow me anyway.

I decided it was time to throw his old
feather duster away. It was getting rather dirty
and smelly and now he had some feathers of his own
he didn't need it to keep him warm.

At first he seemed to miss it.
I think he had imprinted on it as well as on me.
It was already obvious that he
was going to grow up thinking he was human,
but I didn't want him to grow up
thinking he was a feather duster!

Trilby lived inside the house all the time now
(except when I was at school) and to my surprise
Mother had grown to like him very much indeed.
She would often come and talk to him. Trilby
seemed to like her too, but that may have been
because she was usually carrying a feather duster!

More than ever now, Trilby watched
practically everything I did,
and quite often tried to do the same himself.

Each evening he liked to watch the television
with us. It was so funny to see him sitting alone
on a huge chair staring attentively
at the moving pictures on the screen!

Each evening, when I went into the bathroom,
he would hurry in after me and watch intently.
I soon began to realize that he was watching me
so he could learn how to behave.
So, one night, when I had finished washing myself,
I carefully ran just a couple of centimetres
of luke-warm water and placed him gently
in the wash basin.

At once, he started ducking himself into the water,
shaking his head and flapping his wings.
I was surprised to see how much his wings had grown.
They were not puny little stumps any longer,
but beautiful crisp, white feathers.
It would not be long
before he was able to fly.

After he had finished
washing himself,
he hopped onto
one of the taps
and carefully preened
his feathers.

However, one evening he had the most
dreadful accident and almost died.

It was my bath night, and I left Trilby
splashing happily in the wash basin
while I splashed about in the bath.
Then all at once, he decided he wanted a bath too.
He clambered onto the edge of the basin
and flapped over to me.
He landed in the warm, soapy water with a splash
and sank straight underneath.

Hurriedly I fished him out, coughing and spluttering.
He had obviously thought that if it was safe for **me**
in the bath, it must be safe for **him** too!

For the first time, I realized that if birds
imprint on a human they can be placed
in all kinds of danger.

Bird-Spotting Diary

Tuesday May 21st

4.30 p.m.

Today I told the class that when any new feathers sprouted out of Trilby's skin, they were coated with a waxy substance. He spent a long time each day preening this off, so his new feathers could fluff out. He exercised his wings by flapping them vigorously to strengthen the muscles. He couldn't fly but sometimes he would jump off a chair and flap down to the floor - although he wasn't very good at landing!

Mrs Carter said that Trilby's adventures demonstrated some very interesting facts. Although baby birds learn from their parents, they can do many things with no-one to teach them. This is another word beginning with 'I' and we have to find out about it for our homework.

The word is 'instinct'. My dictionary says it is an inborn impulse to behave in a certain way. Trilby could not watch me preening my feathers or trying to fly, yet he knew exactly what to do all by himself.

Instinct tells a bird how to break out of its egg and how to take food from its parents. (So that was why Trilby put his beak in my mouth!) Instinct tells a bird when to migrate and how to build a nest and rear its young. All these behaviour patterns are programmed into the bird's brain. Instincts are inflexible, which means they never change. This is not always in the best interest of a bird. Instinctively, a hen stops laying eggs when she has a clutch of about a dozen and then begins to hatch them. But if the farmer takes them away, she will carry on laying every day!

Chapter Nine

A Letter from Great Aunt Snap

One Saturday, a couple of weeks later,
we were all sitting together in the kitchen
having our breakfast, when Mother
gave a gasp of horror.

"Oh, no!" she groaned, holding up a letter
she had just opened. "Great Aunt Snap has written
to say she's coming to stay with us for a week."

Great Aunt Snap is my mother's Aunt Mildred.
We all call her Great Aunt Snap
because she is so snappy and bad-tempered.
She looks rather like a crocodile
and is the only person in the whole world
that my mother is a little bit afraid of!

"Write and tell the Old Dragon she can't come,"
suggested Dad.

"It's too late," sighed Mum. "She's already
on her way. She should arrive in time for tea.
I'll have to get the guest-room ready
and tidy the house. You know how fussy she is."

"Of course we know," replied Dad.
"Because you take after her!"

"I do not!" snapped Mother.
"I may be just a tiny weeny bit fussy, but I'm not
as bad as her. Last time she complained
that the guest room was disgracefully filthy,
because she found a cake crumb behind the wardrobe!"

"Can Ben and I do anything to help?" asked Dad
(sounding as if he hoped there wouldn't be).

"You can go shopping for me," replied Mother.
"I need several things from the shops for tea.
Make sure you take Trilby with you. Whenever
I'm cleaning, he follows my feather duster
all the time and keeps getting under my feet!"

Both Dad and I were relieved to be spending
the morning out of Mum's way.
So, as soon as she had written out a shopping list,
Dad backed the car out of the garage, and we drove
to the big new supermarket in town.

Trilby had been in the car several times already,
and liked to sit on the back window-ledge.
From there he could see what was going on,
and other drivers could see him.
Sometimes they were so busy staring at Trilby,
that they almost bumped into us!

We parked in the huge car park at the supermarket, and, as we got out of the car, Trilby hopped onto my shoulder. This was now his favourite place, because he hated to have me out of his sight for one single moment.

About half an hour later, we emerged from the supermarket, carrying several heavy shopping bags.

"Do you remember where we parked?" asked Dad, as he stared out across the rows of cars.
"I've forgotten as usual."
"I don't fancy trudging all round the car park with these heavy bags," I groaned.

As we stood there,
wondering what to do next,
Trilby suddenly leapt
off my shoulder and flew out
over the car park.
I was horrified.
Although he was starting
to fly quite well now,
he had never flown
away from me before.
Then, as I wondered
if I would ever see him again,
he landed on the roof of a car
and gave a few shrill squeaks.

"Look!" gasped Dad in astonishment.
"That's our car he's landed on, isn't it?"

It was. It seemed almost unbelievable.
Somehow he had remembered where our car
had been parked, and had managed to recognize it
out of hundreds of others. Was it a coincidence?
If not, how did he do it? Was it instinct again?
Perhaps if Mum knew how useful Trilby could be,
she would let me keep him after all.

But when we got back, I didn't dare ask.
Mother was in a dreadfully bad mood.
"Wipe your feet properly," she scolded.
"And you'd better keep that messy little bird
outside from now on. If Great Aunt Snap
sees one single Billy Bonga in this house,
we'll never hear the last of it."

Bird-Spotting Diary

Saturday June 1st

11.45 a.m.

Trilby found our car in a car park.
I think he did it by instinct.
He knew how to do it without being trained.
My pigeon book has a chapter on Homing Instinct.
It says this is a mysterious ability that pigeons have,
which enables them to find their way home
over long distances.

Trilby is still quite young, and his wings are not strong
enough to fly long distances yet, so he couldn't have flown
back home. Perhaps he is so used to being in the car,
that he thinks of it as a sort of home too. Still, that
doesn't explain everything, because the car can move
around and be in different places. It is very puzzling indeed.
But it did happen. Trilby is certainly no 'Bird Brain'!
Pigeons must be very intelligent! The book says that some
pigeons have found their way home from more than a
thousand miles away. Many years ago, pigeons were used
to carry important messages or letters, tied to their feet.
It was called 'Pigeon Post'!
Trilby is about five weeks old now. He should start
to feed himself soon. The book says young pigeons learn
by watching how their parents and other pigeons feed.

Chapter Ten

One Good Turn . . .

At ten minutes to five that afternoon,
Great Aunt Snap arrived in a taxi.

Mum and Dad opened the front door to meet her.
When they saw that she had two large suitcases,
they exchanged glances and went very pale.

"How nice to see you," gasped Mother,
trying to force a smile.

"Of course it is!" snapped Great Aunt Snap.
"And you'll be glad to hear that I'm staying
for **two** weeks."

Mum looked at Dad and said nothing.
Dad went red in the face and started whistling.
(He always whistles when he feels cross,
and wants to pretend he isn't!)

"Stop that infernal whistling, Harold!"
barked Great Aunt Snap.
"Take my cases upstairs at once.
I hope you've got my tea ready, dear?"

It was odd. Whenever Great Aunt Snap
called anyone 'Dear', the tone of her voice
made it sound like a different word altogether.
As if inside her mind she was calling you
a numbskull or 'muggins'!

We sat down to tea at once,
because Great Aunt Snap was **hungry.**

I looked at my watch. It was almost five o'clock,
time for Trilby's late afternoon feed.

I leaned across the table and whispered to Mum,
"Please may I leave the table?"

"Stop whispering, Boy! It's bad manners!"
shouted Great Aunt Snap, with her mouth full.
"Children should be seen and not heard.
Or even better – **not** seen and not heard!"

Mum glared at me and told me to eat my tea
in silence. Dad winked at me, then had to pretend
he had something in his eye,
when Great Aunt Snap saw him.

I glanced at my watch again and sat there
feeling glum. Trilby had been banned from
the house, so I'd left him shut in the garden shed.
By now he would be getting very hungry and I
could hear faint squeaks through the open window.

Exactly what happened next, I shall never know,
but I imagine that he got impatient
and squeezed out through a hole in the shed door.

Perhaps it was because I hadn't fed him on time,
or perhaps it was the sight of us eating
and drinking, but all at once he decided to try
feeding himself.

Suddenly, just as Great Aunt Snap helped herself
to a huge piece of chocolate cake, Trilby shot in
through the open window and landed on the table.

She dropped her cake on the clean white tablecloth.

She gave a scream that sounded like the noise
a train makes as it goes through a tunnel.
When she finally ran out of breath,
she sat motionless in stunned silence,
her huge mouth hanging wide open.

The slice of chocolate cake landed just in front
of Trilby, and thinking that this kind lady
had given it to him,
he dived upon it
and started to peck up
big beakfuls.
He ate and ate and ate!
Now he knew
how to feed himself,
there was no stopping him.
He got so excited
that he even
stood on the cake,
getting chocolate cream
all over his feet!

Then, feeling thirsty,
he ran over
to Great Aunt Snap's teacup,
leaving a trail
of sticky brown footprints
across the tablecloth.
He perched on the edge
of the saucer,
and stuck his beak
into the piping hot tea.

The boiling hot liquid gave him such a shock
that he leapt off the saucer and ran round
the table with his beak open, right over
everyone's plates.
Finally, he flapped his wings and flew
straight out through the window, dropping a large,
smelly Billy Bonga on Great Aunt Snap as he went!

"**That does it!**" roared Great Aunt Snap.
Her face turned purple,
then she banged her fist on the table and yelled,
"Fetch my suitcases! I'm leaving!
Call me a taxi!"

Five minutes later, she stormed out of the house
and into a taxi without even bothering
to say goodbye.

I sat gloomily at the table
with my head in my hands,
certain that I was in serious trouble.
But worse than that, I realized that Mum would
never let me keep Trilby now. I glanced up at her,
fearing the worst, but to my surprise
she was grinning from ear to ear.

"Three cheers for Trilby!"
she laughed.
"I never thought
we'd get rid
of the old
Snapdragon
that quickly!"

Bird-Spotting Diary

Saturday June 1st

6.15 p.m.

Trilby tried to feed himself today.
As he seems to think that my parents and I are his family,
he watched what we ate, and then tried to do the same.
I thought Mother would be furious, but she wasn't. Even so,
she says it must never happen again, and that I must teach
Trilby to eat proper pigeon food, outside in the garden.

If Trilby had been brought up by his real parents, he would
watch them pecking around on the lawn and copy them.
So I took him outside and scattered some corn
on the grass, then started pecking at it with my nose!
I was dead worried in case any of our neighbours
looked over the fence and thought I was going bonkers.

Trilby just stared at me and seemed very puzzled.
Perhaps he will understand tomorrow,
when he is feeling hungry!

Chapter Eleven

. . . Deserves Another

Things were looking good for Trilby. Mum was so pleased to see the back of Great Aunt Snap, that I was certain she would change her mind and let me keep him. But when I asked her later that evening, I was severely disappointed.

"I thought you liked Trilby now," I moaned.

"I do like him," replied Mother with a sigh. "But I'm also more convinced than ever that pets are messy and cause nothing but trouble. We can't have him running all over the table every time we eat a meal, can we?"
I shook my head.

"He's getting far too messy now," Mum continued. "When he was tiny, he could only make a mess inside his hat, but now that he's bigger he makes messes all over the house. Last night while you were both in the bathroom, he did a Billy Bonga on Dad's toothbrush! When poor old Dad went in to clean his teeth, he thought it was a new kind of toothpaste!"

"He did get rid of Great Aunt Snap for you," I said, trying not to laugh.
"Surely, one good turn deserves another?"

"Maybe," said Mum. "But if Trilby is old enough to feed himself, then he is old enough to live outside.

"From now on he stays in the garden.
But if there's any more trouble, he has to go."

That night I went to bed feeling very miserable.
Trilby slept outside on my bedroom window-sill.
He didn't seem to mind because Mum put her
feather duster on the inside window-ledge,
to cheer him up.

The following morning after breakfast,
I took a handful of corn outside and began
teaching him to eat it. This time he was hungry
and ready to learn.
After he had watched me pretending to peck up
the corn for a while, he had a go himself.
Then I taught him to drink rain water
out of the bird bath.

On Monday, Mother decided that there was no need
for Trilby to go to school with me any longer.
"He's got to start behaving like a real bird,"
she said. "He's spent so much time with humans
that he thinks he is one, which could be dangerous!"
I didn't understand what she was talking about.
What danger could Trilby possibly be in?
He knew how to take care of himself.
He wasn't timid like the other birds in the garden,
who flew off the moment you open the door.

I suppose things worked out fairly well
for the first few weeks. Every morning,
I would sneak out of the front door, while Mum
threw corn on the back lawn to keep Trilby busy.
Then each afternoon, he would sit on the roof
waiting for me. As soon as I appeared
at the end of our road, he would fly down
to meet me, landing on my shoulder.

Then one afternoon he wasn't there.
I stood at the end of the road calling him,
but no wings came flapping in reply.
Something had happened.

I ran home as fast as I could
and burst in through the door.
"Where's Trilby?" I shouted.
"What have you done with him?"

"Calm down," said Mother.

"Trilby has just had a scare,
he's here on the window-sill."

I rushed outside and picked him up.
He was trembling all over.
His feathers were ruffled,
and there was a small smear of blood
on his snowy white breast.

"A cat caught him," Mum explained.
"It leapt out of the bushes while he was pecking
around on the lawn. All the other birds flew away,
but he just stood there."

"The cat pounced on him,
then picked him up in its mouth."

"How did he escape?"

"I saw everything through the kitchen window,"
Mum continued. "I was mopping the floor,
so I shot out of the back door and whacked the cat
with my mop. It was so shocked,
it dropped Trilby and ran off."

"Thanks, Mum," I whispered,
stroking Trilby's ruffled feathers.
"Now I understand why you said Trilby would be
in danger. If he had been brought up by his real
parents, he would have flown away from the cat
like they would."

"Yes," said Mum solemnly. "I'm sorry, Ben, but this
has made up my mind. Trilby needs to be with
other pigeons, or he will never behave like one.
Don't you realize that he will need to find a mate
for himself? He's so confused that he follows
my feather duster instead. On Saturday you can
cycle over to old Mr Dixon's house. He keeps
racing pigeons. You must give Trilby to him."

Bird-Spotting Diary

Thursday 20th June

4.30 p.m.

Today Trilby got caught by a cat. I feel as if it were all my fault. If he had stayed with his real parents it would never have happened. He would have learned to be cautious and fly off at the first sign of danger.

I am beginning to see that when a bird imprints on a human foster parent, it can cause all kinds of problems. Although in one way I saved Trilby's life, my caring for him has now put his life in danger.

Mother is right. He needs to be with other pigeons, so he can learn how to react to predators. He also needs to be with other pigeons, or he will never find a mate.

Trilby is looking quite grown up these days. His tail feathers have grown into a beautiful fan shape. He looks rather like a feather duster himself!

I wish I didn't have to give him away. I shall miss him dreadfully, but it is for his own good. I shall never forget him for as long as I live.

Chapter Twelve

Pigeon Post

Next Saturday morning, I woke up with a horrible
sick feeling in the pit of my stomach.
It was the sort of feeling you get on the morning
of an exam or a trip to the dentist.
But it wasn't either of those things;
it was the day I had to part with Trilby.

After breakfast I sat with him in the garden,
feeding him by hand, stroking his crisp, white
feathers and telling him that everything was going
to work out fine. It was dull and cloudy,
but although the hours passed by,
I just couldn't bring myself to start the journey
to old Mr Dixon's house.

Finally, Mother came out of the house
carrying an old picnic basket.

"Come along, Ben," she called. "You'd better
get going. It's a long way to cycle and I want you
to be back home before it starts to rain."
She handed me the basket and said, "Put Trilby
in here and tie it to the back of your bicycle."

"Trilby isn't used to being shut up," I complained.
"He can travel on my shoulder, like he always does."

"Oh, no, he can't," said Mum, sadly shaking her head.
"He might decide to fly back home. He must stay
in the basket until Mr Dixon shuts him inside
his loft."

"Cheer up," called Mum after me,
as I started pedalling away.
"I expect Mr Dixon will let you visit him."

At the end of the road,
I glanced over my shoulder,
back towards the house.
Mother was still standing
by the gate.
She didn't see me –
she was holding
her handkerchief to her face
and seemed to have
something in her eye.

Mr Dixon lived in the next village.
The journey was a long one, as the road
went right round the old disused slate quarry.
If I could have travelled in a straight line,
I could have been back in less than an hour.

As I passed the old quarry gates,
it started to rain.
I stopped to zip up my anorak hood,
but now I was cycling into the wind
and the icy raindrops stung my face.
Suddenly I had an idea.
I remembered that there was a footpath
across the quarry land.
It was a short-cut to the next village,
but it had been closed off after a landslide.
I knew it was meant to be dangerous,
but surely, if I was careful,
it would be much easier and quicker.

I hid my bike behind some tall brambles.
The gates were padlocked, but there was a small gap
in the fence. I squeezed through it,
carrying the basket with Trilby safely inside.

The path ran along the quarry edge and seemed
perfectly safe, even though it was narrow.
There was a sheer drop of about twenty feet
on one side of it and a steep rocky bank
topped by huge, old trees on the other.

All at once I was startled by a deafening crash
of thunder.

At the same time a dazzling fork of lightning
sparked out of the clouds and struck the rocks
on the bank above, sending them tumbling towards me.
Then, to my horror, the path started to break up.
The last thing I remembered
was holding Trilby's basket above me
and out of danger, before I began to fall
and darkness engulfed me.

I do not know exactly how long I lay unconscious,
but when I eventually woke up, I was lying
in the quarry. I was soaked to the skin
and my right leg was trapped beneath a large boulder.
I tried to move it, but it was impossible.
The pain was unbearable.

I had no doubt: it was broken.
I would have to lie there until I was rescued.

Then I realized I was really in trouble.
No-one knew where I was. Mr Dixon would say
that I had never arrived. Dad would drive
along the road; he wouldn't see my bike
so he wouldn't guess I had crossed the quarry.
It was now getting cold and dark.
I shouted for help, but really I knew
that no-one could possibly hear me.

It was then that I heard Trilby.
A strange, throaty squeak came from the basket.
I peered in at him, relieved to see he was not hurt.

"If only you could fly and get help," I sighed.
Then suddenly I realized, perhaps he could.
His homing instinct should take him back home,
but how could he tell Mum and Dad where I was?

Then I remembered reading in my library book
about the way pigeons used to carry letters.
Pigeon Post, it was called. That was it!
Trilby would carry a message back home
explaining where I was.

I took out my 'Bird-Spotting Diary',
tore out the last page, and I wrote . . .

Help. I have fallen
into the old quarry
and broken my leg.
Please hurry.
Ben.

Carefully, I tied the message to Trilby's leg
with a strand of wool from my scarf.
Then I tossed him into the air
and watched as he flew out of the quarry.

"Go home, Trilby!" I called. "Go home!"
He circled a couple of times
then flew swiftly out of sight.

"I saved you. Now it's your turn to save me."

Bird-Spotting Diary

Saturday June 22nd

7.30 p.m.

I am writing this page in hospital. Trilby saved my life.
I can't write any more. I am exhausted.

Wednesday June 26th

12.30 p.m.

I did break my leg. It has been put in plaster. I have pneumonia
as well, because I lay out in the wind and rain
for almost three hours. Mum and Dad visit me every day,
but it may be a couple of weeks before I am allowed home.
Dad brought me a copy of yesterday's newspaper. There was
a picture of Trilby on the front cover. The headline said:
'Brave Pigeon Saves Boy'. It explained how I had hand-reared
Trilby, and how he had flown home for help after I had fallen
into the quarry. Mum says that Trilby is quite safe.
She and Dad took him to Mr Dixon's house and he is living
inside a pigeon loft. I hope he doesn't mind being shut in.

Friday June 28th

4.30 p.m.

Mrs Carter brought the whole class round
to visit me today, after school.
They all wrote their autographs on my plaster cast.
Mrs Carter drew a picture of a pigeon carrying a message.

I have had lots of get well cards. Mr Dixon sent one.
He says that Trilby has got himself a mate;
a beautiful white fantail pigeon called Leonora.
I am glad. I hope Trilby will be very happy.

Saturday July 6th

I am at home at last. My plaster cast
can't come off for another six weeks but I am quite good
at using crutches. I can't go back to school before
the summer holidays!
But that isn't the best news.

When everyone in the village read in the newspaper
about how Trilby had saved me, they decided to give me
a wonderful surprise . A special sort of pigeon house,
called a dovecote, was made and put in our garden.
Then Mr Dixon brought Trilby back along with his
new mate - Leonora. I can keep them both.

Mum says Trilby is a hero and can live with us
for as long as he likes. She is glad that he has a mate
and behaves like a normal bird!

Epilogue

Tuesday August 27th

This morning, when I went out to feed my two fantail pigeons,
only Trilby came out of the dovecote.
At first I wondered if Leonora was ill.
I peered into the dovecote
and had the nicest surprise yet.
She was sitting
upon two small white eggs.

Trilby is going to be a father!

That means I am going
to have grandchildren!
I must be the youngest grandad
in the whole world!

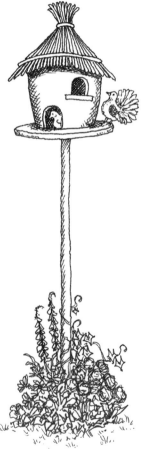